Dear Parent:

Congratulations! Your child is taking the first steps on an exciting journey. The destination? Independent reading!

STEP INTO READING® will help your child get there. The program offers five steps to reading success. Each step includes fun stories and colorful art. There are also Step into Reading Sticker Books, Step into Reading Math Readers, Step into Reading Write-In Readers, Step into Reading Phonics Readers, and Step into Reading Phonics Boxed Sets—a complete literacy program with something for every child.

Learning to Read, Step by Step!

Ready to Read   Preschool–Kindergarten
• big type and easy words • rhyme and rhythm • picture clues
For children who know the alphabet and are eager to begin reading.

Reading with Help   Preschool–Grade 1
• basic vocabulary • short sentences • simple stories
For children who recognize familiar words and sound out new words with help.

Reading on Your Own   Grades 1–3
• engaging characters • easy-to-follow plots • popular topics
For children who are ready to read on their own.

Reading Paragraphs   Grades 2–3
• challenging vocabulary • short paragraphs • exciting stories
For newly independent readers who read simple sentences with confidence.

Ready for Chapters   Grades 2–4
• chapters • longer paragraphs • full-color art
For children who want to take the plunge into chapter books but still like colorful pictures.

STEP INTO READING® is designed to give every child a successful reading experience. The grade levels are only guides. Children can progress through the steps at their own speed, developing confidence in their reading, no matter what their grade.

Remember, a lifetime love of reading starts with a single step!

To Seamus and Oonagh—K.R.

◆

Visit us on the Web!
www.stepintoreading.com
www.randomhouse.com/kids

Educators and librarians, for a variety of teaching tools, visit us at
www.randomhouse.com/teachers

Library of Congress Cataloging in Publication Data
Richards, Kitty.
The great toy escape / by Kitty Richards ; illustrated by the Disney Storybook Artists.
p. cm. — (Step into reading. Step 2)
"Toy story 3."

ISBN 978-0-7364-2662-6 (trade) — ISBN 978-0-7364-8081-9 (lib. bdg.)
I. Disney Storybook Artists. II. Toy story 3 (Motion picture). III. Title.
PZ7.R387Gr 2010 [E]—dc22 2009034687

Printed in the United States of America   10 9 8 7 6 5 4 3 2 1

Disney · PIXAR

TOY STORY 3

The Great Toy Escape

By Kitty Richards

Illustrated by Caroline Egan, Adrienne Brown,
Scott Tilley, and Studio IBOIX

Random House 🏠 New York

Andy's toys love
to play.
But Andy is grown up.
He does not play
with his toys
anymore.

The toys must find
a new home.
They climb
into a car.

The car goes

to Sunnyside Daycare.

Sunnyside is full
of toys!

A bear named Lotso is
in charge.

There are kids
at Sunnyside every day.
Andy's toys are happy.
The kids will play
with them!

But Woody is not happy.

He misses Andy.

He leaves.

It is time to play!

The little kids pull.

They throw.

They yell.

The toys do not like it.

The toys want
to go home.
But the door is locked!

Lotso is mean.

He will not let

Andy's toys leave.

Lotso and his gang lock
up Andy's toys!

Then Woody comes back.

He has a plan.

They will escape!

That night,

Woody and Slinky

steal the key!

The toys sneak outside.
They do not
make a sound.

The toys try to escape.

Oh, no!

They fall

into a garbage truck.

The truck goes
to the dump.
The toys are
in danger!
They must escape.

They run!
Woody tells them
to hurry.
They look
for a way out.

They slide!

The toys hold hands

to stay together.

At last,

they escape!

The toys hide
in the garbage.
They go back
to Andy's house.

The toys are safe.

They are happy

to be home.

Andy finds his toys
a new owner.
She loves to play!
And the toys love
their new home.